Kay dedicates this book to:

Sisters Dorothy Cheek and Sue Solida
Brother Larry Womeldorf
and in Memory of
Brother John Womeldorf

Tessa dedicates this book to:

(Mom), my dog Molly,
and
my friend Devin Zima

CLINKER'S DRAGON

By

Kay Witschen

Illustrated By

Tessa Kay Witschen-Boelz

ISBN-13: 978-0-9741352-2-9
ISBN-10: 0-9741352-2-4

Printed by Professional Office Services, Inc.
Waite Park, MN

Published by Dwitt Publishing
9249 17th St. S.E.
St. Cloud, MN 56304
E-Mail dickawit@aol.com
Website www.dwittpublishing.com

CLINKER'S DRAGON

At the end of a long day of running, chasing and having fun in the forest, Clinker was tired.

"Goodnight everyone. I have to get some sleep. I'll see you tomorrow."

Molly, Spike, Jake, Tory and Zoey said goodnight and started out in all different directions.

At last, thought Clinker, I can get some rest. He hadn't been asleep very long when he heard:

"Clinker, you must wake
You have work to do.
There's no one to help
Save a child except you."

What was that? Clinker did not believe what he was seeing.

It looked like a small dragon.

"Who are you?"

"Can't you see I'm a dragon
I don't often appear
Just when I'm desperately needed
And you have nothing to fear."

"Why do you think **I** need YOU?" asked Clinker.

"A lost little boy
Is not far from here
Your help is needed
There's no one else near."

"What can I do? I don't even know if I believe you. I don't even believe in DRAGONS. Just let me sleep. If you are so smart, you go help him."

"No one else can see me
So it's your help I need
As dogs are loved by children
He will follow your lead."

"Go away," said Clinker. "I'm going back to sleep."

"Please Clinker, I beg you
I would do it if I could
If you do not help him
His chances are not good."

Clinker drifted back to sleep but woke up when something

was tickling his nose.

"Stop that," shouted Clinker. "Get that leaf out of my face!"

*"I know what I've seen
And the boy is not strong
He won't find his way
Unless you come along."*

"O.K. I'll follow you. If you think he'll be so frightened of you, how can you show me the way?"

*"The boy will never see me
I can only be seen by you
Please, please, you must hurry
And trust what I say is true."*

Clinker finally agreed. "Come on, let's get going."

They traveled along for what seemed a long time. Clinker could hardly keep up with the dragon.

"Hey you, whatever your name is, would you slow down. Are you flying or something?"

Then Clinker heard sobs and saw a tiny boy sitting beside a tree. He walked over to the child very slowly, so he wouldn't scare him. When the boy saw him he stopped crying.

"Puppy, puppy," he called. He was smiling now and holding his arms out to Clinker. Clinker went up close enough for the boy to touch. Soon the boy was hugging him and Clinker licked his face.

"If only he will follow
You can take him out of here
He seems to love you already
Just go slow and keep him near."

Clinker started to walk away and the boy giggled and went after him. Clinker stopped every little bit and let him catch up. He did this over and over. Finally he heard the welcome sound of traffic. As they came to the road a police car stopped. The officer got out of the car and went up to the boy.

"Thank heavens you're safe," he said as he picked up the child. "Your Mommy and Daddy and half the town are looking for you."

Clinker started to walk away.

"Hey, dog. If you brought him here you are a real hero."

Clinker was one happy dog as he started to walk back into the woods.

"Now, dragon that I don't believe in, what's your name? You are the real hero."

My friends will **_NEVER_** believe this, thought Clinker, a dragon only **_I_** can see?

The dragon was starting to drift away.

"Goodbye my friend
And by the way
My name is Abigail
You
　　may
　　　　see
　　　　　me
　　　　　　again
　　　　　　　some d a y

Clinker woke up in the morning when he heard his friends talking.

"Listen up Clinker," said Molly. "We have news."

"Come on Clinker," said Zoey. "All over town they are talking about the boy that was found last night."

"Yes," said Tory, "and it sounds like they found him right around here."

"And would you believe it," said Spike, "they said it was a dog that led him out of the woods."

Clinker could not believe what he was hearing. "Wow, that is really something," he said.

"Don't you wish one of us could have been that dog they are calling a hero," said Jake.

So Abigail was really here, thought Clinker. I hope I see her

again some day.

"Come on," yelled Spike. "Whose turn to be it for hide and seek?"

"I guess it's mine," said Clinker, and the other dogs took off running.

"Abigail, wherever you are, you are truly a hero," and a
happy Clinker started off to find his friends.

THE END